Beatrice

Doesn't Want To

For my dearest Nate
L. N.

For Alex, Kendall, and new sister, Lara
L. M.

Text copyright © 1981, 2004 by Laura Numeroff
Illustrations copyright © 2004 by Lynn Munsinger

First edition 2004

Library of Congress Cataloging-in-Publication Data
Numeroff, Laura Joffe.
Beatrice doesn't want to / Laura Numeroff ;
illustrated by Lynn Munsinger. —1st ed.
p. cm.
Summary: On the third afternoon of going to the library with her
brother, Henry, Beatrice finally finds something she enjoys doing.
ISBN 0-7636-1160-3
[1. Libraries—Fiction. 2. Brothers and sisters—Fiction.]
I. Munsinger, Lynn, ill. II. Title.
PZ7 N964 Be 2004
[E]—dc21   2002073908

2 4 6 8 10 9 7 5 3

Printed in China

This book was typeset in Stempel Schneidler.
The illustrations were done in watercolor, ink, and pencil.

Candlewick Press
2067 Massachusetts Avenue
Cambridge, Massachusetts 02140

visit us at www.candlewick.com

Beatrice
Doesn't Want To

Laura Numeroff   illustrated by Lynn Munsinger

CANDLEWICK PRESS
CAMBRIDGE, MASSACHUSETTS

Beatrice didn't like books.
She didn't even like to read.
More than that, she hated
going to the library.

But that's where her brother, Henry,
had to take her three afternoons in a row.
Henry had to look after Beatrice.
He also had to write a report on dinosaurs.

"Why don't you get some books from the shelf?"
Henry suggested when they got to the library.
"I don't want to," Beatrice said.

"Look at how many books there are!"
  Henry said.
"I don't want to," Beatrice repeated.

"Then what do you want to do?"
  Henry asked her.
"I want to watch you,"
  said Beatrice.
"But I have to work,"
  said Henry.
"I'll watch,"
  said Beatrice.

"I give up," said Henry.
He worked on his report.

Beatrice watched.

Henry tried not to notice her.

The second day, Beatrice didn't want to go
back to the library.

"You have to," said Henry.

"I don't want to!" Beatrice told him.

"But I have to work," Henry said.

When they got there,
Beatrice saw a big comfy chair.
"I'll just sit here," she decided.
"Okay," said Henry. "But don't move
until I'm finished."

Henry began to work on his report.

All of a sudden he felt someone tapping his shoulder.

He turned around, and there was Beatrice.

"I'm bored," she said.

"I give up," said Henry.

On the third day,
Beatrice followed Henry
around while he looked
for more books.

"Can I hold some?" Beatrice asked.
Henry gave her some books to hold.

"They're too heavy," Beatrice wailed.
"I really do give up," said Henry.
"You're driving me crazy!"

"Please, Bea," Henry begged her.
"I've got to get this report done.
It's due tomorrow."

"How about a drink of water first?"
said Beatrice.

They went down the hall to look for some water.
Suddenly Henry saw a poster.

This is *it*!
he thought.

The librarian will read
ALBERT MOUSE HAS
A BRAND-NEW HOUSE
today at 4:00 P.M.
in the children's room

"Come on," said Henry.
"I don't want to," answered Beatrice.

"Too bad!" shouted Henry.

Before Beatrice knew it,
she was in a room full of other children.
Henry walked out just as she started
to say, "I don't want —"

Beatrice sat down to wait for Henry.
"Hello. My name is Wanda," said the girl
in the next chair. "This is the second
time I've heard this story."
"Big deal!" said Beatrice.

"'Albert Mouse lived in a
brand-new house,'" the
librarian began to read.
She held the book up
so everyone could
see the pictures.

Beatrice glared
out the window.

"'Albert Mouse also had new roller skates,'" the librarian continued.

Beatrice loved to roller-skate.
She looked at the librarian.

" 'But Albert's mother wasn't too thrilled when he skated through the house,' " the librarian read.

The boys and girls laughed. Beatrice smiled.

She remembered the time she had tried
roller-skating in her own house.
Then Beatrice laughed.
She listened to the whole story.

When the story was over,
Beatrice went up to the librarian.

"May I see that book, please?" she asked.
"Of course," said the librarian.

Beatrice sat down and looked at
each picture over and over.

Suddenly she felt someone tapping her shoulder.
"Time to go," Henry whispered.

Beatrice kept looking
at the pictures.

Henry stuck Beatrice's hat on her head.
"We have to go home now," he said.

Beatrice ignored him.
"Come on, Bea," Henry said.

"I don't want to," Beatrice said.